Prime Sensations

LIANA BROOKS

OTHER WORKS

Find other works by the author at
http://www.lianabrooks.com

HEROES AND VILLAINS

Even Villains Fall In Love
Even Villains Go To The Movies
Even Villains Have Interns
Even Villains Play The Hero (books 1 – 3 omnibus)

TIME AND SHADOWS MYSTERIES

The Day Before
Convergence Point
Decoherence

NEWTON'S LAWS

Bodies In Motion
Change of Momentum (forthcoming)
For Every Action (forthcoming)

Prime SENSATIONS

LIANA BROOKS

AUSTRALIA

This story first appeared as 'Prime Sensations' in the *Tales from the SFR Brigade* anthology, 2013.

This is a work of fiction. All characters, organisations and events are the author's creation, or are used fictitiously.

Print ISBN: 978-1-925825-71-8
eBook ISBN: 9781386895015

www.inkprintpress.com

National Library of Australia Cataloguing-in-Publication Data
Brooks, Liana 1982—
Prime Sensations
94 p.   cm.
ISBN: 978-1-925825-71-8
Inkprint Press, Canberra, Australia
1. Science fiction 2. Space colonies—Fiction 3. Romance fiction
4. Science fiction—Women authors

Summary: Kaleb thought Lana died years ago in the war, but now they're together again and teaming up for the heist of the century.

Second Edition: August 2018

"Unidentified vessel, we are Waste Hauler 133 out of Darrian 6. We carry no trade or crew," the ship's AI droned in a bored monotone.

Lana dropped into the waste hauler's modified control booth and took over. "Unidentified vessel, be advised. I steer like a drunken moose, alter your course." The reverb over the frequently patched comm lines made her sound like an old man with a lifelong bitter-root habit.

Sweat dripped down her nose. The waste hauler had a hull thirty years older than she was, and an environmental system older than that. It had survived two major system wars by being too worthless to target. And Lana was well aware that, as a debtor working off her ransom to the Iloni nation, she was slightly less valuable than the ship.

The comm crackled and she thought she heard the word "boarding."

"Unidentified vessel, I am deaf and blind. I give you no authorization to come near this vessel. If you keep to your projected course I will have no choice but to heartlessly smash your hull because of physics."

The other ship tried to respond.

Lana grimaced and tried to compensate for the ancient communications array. "Mass times acceleration, unidentified vessel. I can't slow down in time."

"Waste Hauler 133, this is the *Marsail* out of Port Tael, flying the flag of the Exaner Confederation. Prepare to be boarded."

Black holes and dark nights! Port Tael was a pirate station, taken by the outer rim unification during the Apex War, and currently under stars only knew which warlord.

She leaned against the rough metal of the control booth. They probably wanted to pick over the hauler for parts. Stars knew there was enough wreckage welded in to rebuild a fleet. She should probably get dressed.

Lana sniffed her armpit. Maybe a shower was in order. And clothes. And snacks. The *Marsail* wouldn't cross paths with her hauler for a few more hours, and it was the most exciting thing to happen since she'd been taken as a prisoner of war three years ago.

The *Marsail* managed to land on the bulky waste hauler with a finesse Lana would have envied a few years ago, back when she'd thought her rift rat piloting skills would be enough to win the attention she craved.

It never had.

She tossed a boiled nut into her mouth and watched the pirate crew's slow progress through the hull. If there'd been someone to bet against, she would have wagered they'd go for the hard metals compartment, maybe grab some radiated shielding or a new engine converter.

Her second bet was the food waste department, where they might try panning for seeds. Not that it would do them any good—the Iloni poisoned the food waste to ensure the vegetation of Darrian 6 wasn't sold on the black market—but they were welcome to try.

The enemy ship latched on like a leech and sliced through her hull. The crew moved methodically toward the control deck.

If she'd had a weapon, she would have gone out to meet them. The only gear worth having was the bits she'd salvaged. Not enough to build a shuttle, not yet, but in another year or three she'd have a means of escape. If they took that...

Lana eyed the console and considered the maneuvers she'd need to shake the smaller ship off. Scrapping them against the mine corridor that kept her from diverting off course sounded promising. She was running over the possible course corrections needed when someone banged on the door of the control booth.

"Pilot?" The person hammered on the door again. "Waste Hauler Pilot, open this door."

She raised an eyebrow and grabbed another boiled nut. Telling the intruder she'd survived far worse than they could dish out was a waste of oxygen. Right now, she was breathing. If that changed in the next few minutes, no one was going to care, least of all her.

"Open this door or we will open it for you."

"Be my guest."

"Stand back."

She looked around at the cramped booth, a cylinder of buttons, viewing screens, and control panels. Given enough time and the right tools, she could rip out the main radar and stuff herself into the box, but that would take at least an hour. The door in front of her radiated heat.

Lana lifted the chair that had long ago rusted loose just in time to prevent hot metal shrapnel from hitting her face. "Hi." She set the chair down so she could look into the black faceplate of her attacker. With a smile, she slapped the panic button that sent the waste hauler into a death spiral, alarm beacons screaming. "Iloni forces will be here within the hour. Do you want to shoot me now, or later?" The increased gravity of the spiral pulled at her. For a moment it looked like her attacker planned on retreating. She winked at the black face mask. "Pretty girl got your tongue?"

The invader pushed past her, boots scrapping along the floor, and fumbled to hit the bypass code with large hands. "You think I don't know that trick?"

"Do you think I care what you know?"

The faceplate cleared as he turned to her. And Lana found herself staring into the shocked eyes of Kaleb Hath—the man who'd left her for dead.

Lana's nails bit into her palms as her fists clenched. "Commander Hath, if I'd known it was you, I would have vented my oxygen an hour ago."

Kaleb swore behind his faceplate. "Our information said Rear Commander Daniels was on this vessel." He'd been expecting a craggy octogenarian with a tactical mind second to none, not the woman who haunted his dreams. His eyes flicked to the oxygen stats on his body armor. Everything was operating under normal parameters, so why did he feel like his head was about to float out the space lock?

Dark eyes narrowed. "Leave, before I start the decompression sequence."

"I'm wearing armor, Lana. You can't kill me with decompression." His fingers twitched as he fought the urge to strip his armor off and run his hands across her body to assure himself it really was her. Stars, it had been so long. She looked so thin, so…beaten.

"But I *can* kill myself, which would mean never seeing you again. We'd both be happy."

He stiffened. "I would never hurt you."

"Really? Dropping my team into the middle of a training ground to pick up your weapons wasn't a suicide mission? The fact that you could only make one pass and only picked up *your* soldiers wasn't accidental at all?"

"That was your call, not mine." He'd gone over it again and again in his mind. Reliving the drop, the fire fight, and that single pass when he'd tried to pull everyone out. But they'd only had one dropship left, and Lana was team leader. "You opted to stay behind so everyone else could get out."

Lana turned away from him. "I thought you'd come back, but I guess I didn't mean enough to you." She dropped into the pilot's seat. "Take what you want, then get out. Run back to your pretty little farm, and your fawning little lieutenant. I'm not fighting your war anymore."

Kaleb's throat went dry. The soft feedback of his breathing was the only sound. "The war's over, Lana."

"Congratulations. I don't care what you did to the Iloni. I won't work with Quintus again."

"The war was over before we hit that supply depot. By the time we broke out of there, the Iloni had won."

She looked back at him, large brown eyes wide with confusion. "What? How's that even possible?"

"Do you remember the rockets they had? The ELE Terrorizers?"

"Extinction Level Event..." He saw her thoughts catching up with his words. "They wouldn't dare. They couldn't!"

"They did. Every single outer planet sent into nuclear winter. Over ninety percent of the population wiped out. We're all pirates now, stealing what we can, and starving when we can't grab enough."

Lana gave him a withering look. "And you thought the Rear Commander would somehow provide a miracle? I haven't seen another living human being in three years and I'm already regretting this encounter. Can't you and the rest of the species go die without me?"

"I have the miracle. I just need a strategy to steal it." Kaleb smiled. "What do you say, Lana? One more heist, for old time's sake?"

A gray shirt, too large to be flattering, and olive drab pants that were too short for the name replaced Lana's yellow coveralls. No one alive could make the combination look flattering, but after years of wearing the same rough fabric, the clothes from the *Marsail* felt like butter against her skin.

Squeezing the last of the water from her freshly washed hair, Lana took a deep breath.

Clean air. Clean, cool, recycled, and properly recharged air.

It smelled like Kaleb, black holes and darkest night take him. Seeing him again made the memories of their raid on the Prenta Compound of Darrian 5 resurface like toxic gas bubbling up from a swamp.

There had been times when she'd screamed herself awake, shouting for someone to take cover. But it was the memories of the nights spent with Kaleb on the planet Quintus that stole her breath and turned her blood to ice.

She'd been a gunner on the pirate ship *Teela's Revenge*. Their captain had led a successful raid on one of the Iloni agro ships that orbited near the third planet; plants, seeds, three holds full of food ready to be shipped to the Iloni home world.

Captain Fidela traded regularly with the Quintus government, and the haul had been worth a celebration. Kaleb had been there, handsome in his dress white uniform, and strikingly different.

Lana forced herself to check her image in the small mirror of her berth. The woman in the reflection was a gaunt wraith compared to the woman she'd once been. With a glare, she reminded herself that appearance didn't matter. Looks had gotten her into this mess.

That party. Kaleb watching her across a crowded room; she feeling self-conscious because she'd run out of the bleach needed to dye her hair Outer Planets Pale. Her dark hair and eyes tattled on her. Everyone knew she was an Iloni bastard. Some wanted to take her as an exotic conquest. Most avoided her. Kaleb had caught her eye and winked.

He had the same dark hair and eyes as she, but *his* personality turned him from pariah into exotic godling. Everyone loved Kaleb. He was charming, he was witty, he was smart, he was carved out of muscles, and tasted like Melinian spiced wine. She, the rift rat without polish or charm who stumbled through every conversation, had gotten drunk on his attentions. Within weeks, she'd invited him to bed.

They'd become lovers, and then partners in war when the *Revenge* signed onto the pact. She'd voted for that. The Iloni needed to be stopped, the Outer Planets needed to retain their sovereignty. And joining the Apex War meant spending more time with Kaleb.

Darkest night, but there were days she wanted to slap her younger self silly.

She stepped into the corridor and looked around. The *Marsail* was an old Radial-style ship. *Teela's Revenge* had been a Radial-238, with holds and berths on the outer circle, engines and common areas in the center, and a control level and guns sandwiched between the two ends. More hours than she could recall had been spent running laps around the central engine core.

The *Marsail,* though, looked like a Radial-Dima model. Instead of a control level there was an elongated core running through the axis of the ship. Walking into the common room, she didn't see the core access. But Kaleb was there.

He stood, smiling. She turned away, shutting him out. Feigning interest in the computers, Lana pulled up information on the war. She'd guessed there was an end in sight when the ransom notice came, but to use the ELE bombs? The pictures on file were horrific. Entire planets' ecosystems reduced to ash. Starving survivors and frozen victims.

People began shuffling in. They walked past her, muttering. "Iloni," as in times past, was a favorite word. The accents were from all over the outer rim of the solar system. She even caught a few phrases delivered in rift rat cant.

And through it all she could feel Kaleb watching her. His stare heated the back of her neck. Lana rubbed it, and flipped him an obscene gesture. Her reward was a soft baritone chuckle.

Three years ago it would have led to him coming over to whisper in her ear. Whispers would have turned to flirting, then flirting to kissing—and she would have woken up the next morning naked in his arms.

Lana glanced at the dark monitor beside her. Kaleb's reflection still watched her, his eyes filled with the same combination of desire, regret, and loss that she knew too well. How many times had he looked at her like that before a mission? How many times had he kissed her goodbye and begged her to come back safe? It hurt to know that look so well, to know exactly what he was feeling with nothing more than a glance. She bit the inside of her cheek to keep herself from smiling at him. He'd left her for dead. He hadn't even tried to save her. Whatever had been between them had been fun, but three years as an Iloni prisoner had confirmed all her worst fears. No matter what Kaleb might have said, he had never truly loved her.

"That's not Daniels," a nasal female voice said, just in case someone had mistaken Lana for the ancient general.

She turned in surprise. "Geana?"

The Melinian mercenary draped herself over Kaleb's shoulder, fine golden hair all but glowing. "I thought you were dead." Her smug tone suggested that since Lana was now inconveniently alive, death could be arranged.

Kaleb tried to shrink away from Geana, but it didn't work. She clung to him.

Lana shot back. "I guess being a mercenary wasn't enough. You've taken up whoring while I was away?" Melinians didn't usually sail with mixed-race crews for merc work, but Geana might have signed on as Ship's Counselor, as they liked to call the captain's prosti.

Geana shrugged, a graceful movement any goddess would envy. "You know me. I'd do anything for cash."

"Or anyone," Lana muttered, shooting a dark look at Kaleb. She'd read him wrong after all. That hadn't been loss and desire in his eyes; it had probably been Geana-induced fatigue. With a toss of her head, Lana turned back to the computer console, her braid slapping the back of her chair with a wet thwack. Score one for the mercenary. Rift rats weren't pretty, just functional.

Kaleb cleared his throat. "Now that we're all here, we need to discuss what we're doing."

"We're going home!" someone shouted from the far side of the room. "Daniels was the key to this. We can't pull it off without him."

"Rear Commander Daniels would have been an asset. The information on where he was imprisoned was outdated. The good news is we found Lana instead. She was a gunner and combat team leader on *Teela's Revenge*. You know the *Revenge's* reputation. Some of you have fought with Captain Fidela's pirates, so you know this isn't a bad trade."

Not a bad trade. She snorted and focused furiously on catching herself up on the news, tuning Kaleb out and filling herself in on the current political situation. Leaving the waste hauler was beginning to look like a huge mistake.

"We don't need Daniels for this," Kaleb continued. "The original plan still holds." The lights in the room dimmed as he turned on the holograms, but she refused to look. "The Iloni High Command has traditionally kept the Nova Crystals at an undisclosed location on Darrian 6. Even during the height of the war, our intelligence network could never pinpoint their location. Six weeks ago, they were moved to a display for the Imperator's birthday celebration."

There were gasps around the room.

Lana snuck a glance at the hologram of Darrian 6. A string of brightly-colored terraforming gems stretched from Prime orbital space station down to the Iloni capital city. Each Nova Crystal was a different color, and some were larger than the asteroid fragments she'd collected as a miner. Even in the muted light of the holo-projection, the crystals glowed like a summer rainbow, full of hope and promise. A single Nova Crystal could terraform a planet in under a decade. It was the technology that had allowed humanity to settle the Outer Planets. The crystals hadn't been on display in centuries. Stars above! The Imperator might have spelled out an obscene message with solar flares with less trouble. The Outer Planets weren't dead yet, and she hoped she'd have a chance to ram that fact down the Imperator's throat one day.

"Prime Orbital is too well guarded for our team to enter. It's the primary control point for the nexus web that holds the Nova Crystals on display, and only full-blooded Iloni from ruling families are allowed there."

Someone nearby muttered, "Pleasure dome."

"Exactly. The Iloni might not be very empathetic but they like their vices as much as anyone," Kaleb said. "We can't get in there. Below is the secondary entry point." The light flickered as the holo-projection changed to an image of a dull-looking green building on Darrian 6. "The tethers are here, and this is where the cleaning crews enter. The nexus web needs regular cleaning, and the crews change out daily. We'll put a team in as a cleaning crew, grab one of the patrol ships tethered there, and swoop out with the Nova Crystals."

"It won't work," said a business-like voice. Lana was surprised to find it was hers.

Kaleb looked across the room at Lana's back. Geana squeezed his hand in a bid for his attention, but he ignored her. "What do you mean, it won't work? It's simple. It gets us to the objective. We have the element of surprise in our favor. What could go wrong?"

Lana swiveled her chair around. "Everything?" Light from the computer played over her face, accenting the sharp angles. "If you do a smash and grab, nothing is going to stop the Iloni from pursuing you. And what about the primary power source for the nexus web? You think you can wish it away?"

"The nexus web cycles through sequences on a timer. They all do. There's always a reset when the secondary power source is holding up the web. We can get to the secondary power source, so that's the one we target. We get in, take down the power source, and snatch the Nova Crystals during a reset."

Lana shook her head. "You think no one will notice that?"

"Do you have a better idea?"

He couldn't see her well in the dark, but he knew Lana like he knew his own heartbeat—she was rolling her eyes.

"Don't I always?"

Kaleb smiled, too ready to pounce on her familiar offer to hide his pleasure at the way she fell into the well-worn roles they'd established years ago. When they'd worked as an insertion team on raids it had always been like this. He'd find an idea, she'd perfect it.

And when they were done plotting their raids, they put their skills to use in the bedroom. Or the shower. Or…

A shiver crawled down his spine as Lana stepped into the light of the holo-projector. From the scowl on her face, he knew her thoughts weren't aligned with his.

He took a step back, inhaling the cold ship air and refocusing himself. "What would you suggest?"

Lana's finger trailed through the light of the holo-projector, changing the view so they could see Prime Orbital, the gems, and the capital of Darrian 6. "We need three teams. A small team hits Prime. The primary power source can't be altered by computer, but it *can* be physically disconnected. Unless the Iloni have changed in the past three years, it's going to be a connection that's easily reachable for fast repairs. They like to keep things simple."

"It'll be guarded," Geana predicted. She leaned against Kaleb.

He crossed his arms.

Lana's gaze flickered to them and then turned back to the layout. "Prime is the only guard they need. No one gets up there unless they have the name, rank, and cash. You'd never get in," she added with a catty smile aimed at Geana. "Your pale hair would mark you right away."

"I could be a sex worker," Geana said.

Lana shook her head. "You've never tried to crash Prime. We looked at it. It's a treasure trove—a pirate's wet dream—but we didn't have enough Iloni bastards on the *Revenge* to make it work. Genetic contracts in the upper levels of the Iloni are arranged by the Imperator himself. Prime is where people go with their high-bred lovers when they want to avoid their legal spouses. The only people allowed up there are Iloni. Even the workers are Iloni purebreds."

"It's not legally adultery if it happens on Prime," Kaleb translated for the rest of the crew. Most of them were Outer Planets born or rift rats, and of the crew, he was certain Geana, Lana, and himself were the only ones who'd ever worked the inner system.

Geana looked at him. "Who cares if they have an affair if they have an arranged marriage for kids? You can have sex without getting knocked up."

"It's considered treason." He shrugged. "Don't look at me like that, I didn't make the rule."

Lana tapped her finger on the console. "With a fake or stolen ID, I can get in. I've passed for true Iloni on other raids." She flicked the layout to focus on the crystals and the patrol ships tethered around there. "Stealing an Iloni ship to grab the Nova Crystals is a good idea. There's no way we can get another ship past the perimeter, but we need the *Marsail* in position near the rift. Team two is going to handle the actual grab. You'll need to get in as workers, get in position, and move in unison to untether or destroy the ships while the main ship grabs the crystals."

"What about the nexus web?" someone asked.

"I'll shut off the primary power, and the second team will turn the secondary power to forty percent. The alarm cutoff is around thirty or thirty-five, but forty is low enough that the power levels won't trigger an alarm, and that the nexus web will fail within minutes of the primary source getting cut."

"Where's the third team?" Geana asked.

Lana switched the display to show the Outer Planets. "Here. Do you think the Iloni will let you stroll away with the Nova Crystals and offer no retribution? Do you think they'll let you terraform the Outer Planets? The Iloni will destroy you, every last one of you. The Imperator won't care how many ships he loses. All that will matter will be reducing the Outer Planets to atoms, and you along with it. There'll be nothing left to terraform. We need every available ship in the outer system to reduce the Iloni long-range capacity to ash."

Kaleb sucked his breath in between his teeth. "You're talking about war. A second Apex War."

The light from the console flickered as Lana moved. "Do you want your farm or not, Hath?"

Lana retreated from the common room, hands shaking. Darkest night take Kaleb, she hadn't meant to say anything. She was just along for the ride. But that was their thing. He made an offer, she countered with something better, and then he was supposed to polish it off. Not turn it on her and make her accountable for dragging the Outer Planets back to war.

The door to her berth slid closed behind her and she collapsed onto the cold bed. Even her pillow smelled like Kaleb. She pushed herself up and then picked it up to sniff it again. It was in her imagination. Everything here reminded her that he was on the ship.

She lay back down, trying to remember the last time she'd been so nervous in front of a man. *Right.* When she'd first met Kaleb. He wasn't ashamed of what he looked like. He'd told her fellow gunner Ambris that he liked his dark hair, because it made him unique. The night she'd gone after him, she'd spent over an hour primping in the mirror, hoping he'd find her beautiful instead of freakishly abhorrent.

And now they were back at square one, planning to go to war.

She replayed the scene from the common room in her mind. Was there a better plan? A better way? She couldn't see one.

The Outer Planets needed those crystals, and if they wanted to rebuild without the Iloni destroying their worlds again, they had to eliminate the fleet's long range capabilities. No one had ever tried to take the inner system; no one wanted to overthrow the Imperator, except maybe the lower class Iloni. But the Outer

Planets, with hundreds of years of individual sovereignty? It made sense they'd want it back.

There was a knock at her door. Kaleb, no doubt, come to apologize or beg or whatever it was old lovers did when they didn't want to get shot in the back because they'd abandoned you and left you to die.

"Go away."

The door slid open. Geana leaned against the doorframe. "Am I interrupting your beauty sleep?"

Lana pulled the pillow over her face. "Space yourself, Geana."

"He mourned for you, did you know that?"

"Do you need a handwritten card to get the message? I don't want to talk to you. At all." Lana lifted the pillow and glared. "Can you even read? I don't want to waste my time writing a note if you can't read."

"He spent a year in mourning when you were lost," Geana repeated.

"We lost a lot of people on that mission. I wasn't the only one he was mourning." *He wasn't mourning me at all, the rat bastard.*

"He hasn't taken another woman to his bed since. I know. I like to scout out my competition, but I was fighting a ghost."

"Kaleb doesn't ever take women to bed. He likes to be chased. Try seducing him. You'll get a better reaction."

Geana chuckled. "You think I didn't try that? Me? Come on, Lana, that was my move before you even had your first orgasm."

Lana sat up. "What do you want?"

"Kaleb."

She shrugged. "Hooray? What do you want me to say here? He's not mine. I don't want him. If you have a murder fetish and want a lover who will dump you at the first sign of trouble, more power to you. Personally, I think you could find starfish that make better lovers, but that's just my opinion."

"Kaleb would have been in my bed within the week, except you're back and instead of pining for a ghost, he's daydreaming of you. He's up on the command deck right now. He wants to talk to you, and what do you want to bet that he's going to offer to come climbing right back into your bed?"

Lana looked around. "A pillow?" She held it out for Geana to take.

"What?"

"I bet you a pillow that Kaleb won't be my lover ever again." She shrugged. "Sorry, it's all I have." She shook the pillow. "I'm betting everything I own that I will never be stupid enough to trust Kaleb Hath again. Does that satisfy you? Will you go strip him down and knock tumblies together now?"

Geana sneered. "Tell *him* that. Because until he hears it from you, he's going to keep feeding his fantasy and I'm not going to get a tumble at all." She raised an eyebrow. "He *is* waiting in the control room, by the way. As soon as your beauty rest is over, you should get up there and polish up this master plan of yours."

Lana growled. "Fine. I'll go tell him, then he can go hop on over to you while I do the work. Does that suit you?"

"Sounds fabulous." Geana gestured for her to move. "Ladies first."

Lana rolled her eyes and stalked toward the common room before remembering that this wasn't a Radial-238 and she had no idea how to access the control room.

"It's a Revolve-9," Geana called after her. "The access ladder is down the recline hall."

The ship designer must have been on drugs to put an access hatch in the recline hall, but that's where it was, half way down the slanted corridor that could unfold as a ramp if large equipment on this level needed to be replaced. She climbed the ladder, cursing silently, and stepped into the dimly lit control room. Kaleb sat hunched over the central screen.

Adrian Hatheron di Vera—the name glowed in yellow letters on Kaleb's screen. He touched the screen, pulling up a picture of an Iloni nobleman dressed in the uniform of the Imperator's elite personal guard. Beneath di Vera's pedigree, the pilfered documents listed his education, accomplishments, and the subsequent disgrace that had resulted in a life sentence of servitude. A lesser-born Iloni would have found himself mining asteroids or burning to death on the farms of Darrian I, but not di Vera. No. The Imperator had outdone himself on that one. Di Vera was serving as a gladiator in the pleasure domes of Prime Orbital.

Rear Commander Daniels would have understood; he had been the only one who'd listened when Kaleb suggested exploiting the growing rift between the Imperator and the wealthy families of Darrian 6. For some reason Kaleb couldn't picture his Outworld crew understanding why Adrian was important.

Behind him the door shushed open and closed. He turned to see Lana stepping into the blue glow of the safety lights.

Kaleb licked his lips as a thousand thoughts flew through his mind. "I'm sorry." The words tumbled past his lips. "I told Geana to let you sleep."

She shrugged, looking at Adrian rather than him. "The sooner we finish this, the sooner I'm rid of you." Lana glared at him. "I don't want you."

"Lights." He tried not to frown as the room brightened. Amid the lush red couches and gold trim of the stolen luxury yacht, Lana looked like a whipped slave. Still, as she glowered at him in defiance, he couldn't help but remember all the reasons he'd fallen in love with her.

"You don't want me to what?"

"I don't want to be lovers again. I don't trust you."

Kaleb's eyebrows went up in surprise, then he schooled his face into a more neutral reaction. He hadn't expected her to jump back in bed with him today, or tomorrow, or ever... if he was honest. No matter how much he wished it otherwise. "Fine." He turned back to the screen. "Are you going to help me with this?"

She walked over to the plush seat opposite him. "Geana said you were pining for me."

"Try to remember that Geana comes from a planet where mind games are after-dinner entertainment. Don't let her mess with your head." He pulled up a map of the inner system.

"After everything we had, that's all you have to say?"

He could see her biting her lip in the reflection in the screen next to him. He wanted to pull her close, promise her anything, but... She didn't want him?

Fine.

He swallowed the emotions and put on his commander's face. "What do you want me to say? You've said you don't want to be my lover. Fine. You've said you don't trust me. Fine. It's all crystal clear, but it doesn't change anything that's happening over the next eight days. Believe it or not, I wasn't sitting up here lusting after your body. I'm trying to save the only place in the universe where I'm welcome." He took a deep breath. "Maybe you don't care about us. We have no reason to ask anything of you, least of all me, but please? I need your help, even if you don't want anything to do with me."

Her cheeks flushed. "Sorry. I should have…" She waved her hand to clear the air. "Never mind. Let's pretend we've never met and just… work."

"Work is good." He sent a timetable for the raid to her screen.

She made alterations and sent it back.

They worked quietly, changing the main holo-projection so they could see the angles, and making their plans in silence. Slowly the plan to take Prime Orbital formed. Teams were set for the ground assault, transport, and a skeleton crew that would proceed to the Outer Planets to call up help. Lana placed herself on the Orbital insertion team.

The thought of her going alone into Iloni territory made his blood run cold. "You do need me."

"What?" Lana jerked back as if slapped.

"The team on Prime Orbital needs at least two people. I'm the only other person who can pass for true blooded Iloni. You may not want me, but you do need me."

Green safety lights illuminated the narrow path that separated the cargo hold from the engine core. Kaleb swore, and pushed himself to complete another lap. Running down here, where the ship's gravity was strongest, was a habit he'd picked up from Lana. She'd run on the *Revenge*, and when they'd become lovers he'd joined her for morning jogs.

He sagged against the wall at the halfway point, mentally kicking himself for thinking of Lana.

Unbidden, the image of the explosion that had stolen her from him bloomed in his mind's eye. The shuttle was overloaded, smoke from the battle jammed his sensors, and she'd told him to go…

"Get out of here, Kaleb."

"I can't leave you."

"You can't take me with you."

"I'll come back."

"I love you…"

They hadn't even made low orbit when the ground beneath them became a chrysanthemum of fire. When the peace treaty was signed—a hollow gesture that bought a few years of freedom for the survivors—Lana's name had been listed among those killed in action.

Kaleb dropped his head back against the metal bulkhead. If he'd known… If he'd only known.

Footsteps, light and even, echoed in the darkness.

He pulled himself back into the alcove where emergency gear would have gone if they weren't running such a bare bones operation. Lana jogged into view wearing the same olive and gray combination as the rest of the crew—but on her it looked good.

More footsteps followed, heavier and out of rhythm.

Lana stopped not far from his hiding spot. In the dim light he saw fear on her face.

"Lana," he called softly.

She spun around, eyes wide as her hand dropped to her thigh. She pulled her knife from its sheath.

"Problems?" Kaleb asked as he stretched and stood up.

"Hey there." Andre Jorgenson rounded the corner with his friend Raul. He choked. "Captain."

Lana stepped closer to him, her hand white-knuckled around the hilt of her knife.

Kaleb raised an eyebrow. "I didn't know you'd taken up running, Andre. I thought the gravity down here was a little too much for you to stomach."

Andre coughed again and looked at Raul. "Um, no, sir. We, ah, just came down to, ah, run laps."

Kaleb stepped forward and patted Andre on the back a little harder than was friendly. "You came down here to run, not corner anyone and give them a hard time because they're an Iloni bastard?"

"No, sir," was Andre's too quick response.

"So glad to hear it. I've been looking for running partners. Lana." He saluted her and gave the boys a light push on their backs.

Six laps later, after running Andre and Raul until they puked, he was still seeing red. Lana had never, ever been scared. He'd done that to her. No one on that team knew better than he what tortures the Iloni could dish out. And he'd left her for them.

Gasping for air, Kaleb leaned against the bulkhead and plotted a way to give Lana her confidence back.

"I look like an idiot." Lana glared at him from under several fashionable layers of Iloni makeup.

"You're the Iloni epitome of beauty, I assure you."

"The Iloni are idiots."

Kaleb ran a hand over the flounced lime green skirt that was currently the height of masculine fashion on Darrian 6. "I'm not arguing with you on that one."

Lana glowered at him, but her eyes were smiling.

"Do I look utterly ridiculous?"

She laughed. "Yes." She tried to sit down on the courtesy shuttle bench, but gave up. The bright red dress she wore obscured half her face with a high neckline and stabbed down into a sharp, starched hem along her leg. "I don't even know how to sit in this. We're going to be arrested because someone will ask me to sit and I won't know how."

He chuckled. "Don't worry, the IDs are flawless." Authentic too, but since Lana had trusted him with the details of getting them into Prime while she organized the rest of the crews, he didn't feel the need to weigh her down with the nitty gritty details. If the Imperator knew Kaleb Hatheron di Vera was walking the halls of Prime, the man would have a heart attack.

The shuttle glided into the launch space and docked with a click.

"Show time." Kaleb fanned their IDs and then tucked them in his shirt pocket. Lana tossed her hair. Haughty as the Imperator's daughter, she glided toward the gene scanner and stretched out her hand. The small pad lit up blue.

"Welcome, Lana si Vera," a computerized voice said as the doors to the station slid open.

"Who is Lana si Vera?"

Kaleb scanned his hand. "The new wife of Kaleb Hatheron di Vera," he said over the computer's welcome.

"We've come to Prime as newlyweds? You don't think someone will find it off?"

He brushed the hair out of her face as the lock cycled shut behind them. "Newlyweds come to Prime. Besides, if we were here as established lovers people would expect certain behaviors. An arranged marriage is the perfect excuse for our less than..." He fumbled for a word.

"For the fact that you can't look me in the eye?" Lana supplied tartly. The lock to Prime station opened. Lana marched ahead, commanding attention as she stepped into the bustle of the main atrium.

Kaleb lingered, watching her and wondering if her acidic reply was an invitation or a warning.

When the crew of *Teela's Revenge* had discussed Prime, it had been with wild speculation based on a pirate's ideas of a good time. "Somehow, I expected more nudity," Lana said, Kaleb stepping close to view the atrium where low lights illuminated a warm jungle scene.

Kaleb switched their luggage to his other hand. "This is the entry level where we check in. Note how the shrubbery conveniently hides all the other docking bays."

"I thought the plants were here to filter the air."

"Nope, they're here so spouses aren't embarrassed by seeing each other when they visit with someone else." He held out his hand. "Can you do this for a few hours?"

Hesitantly, she touched him, letting her fingers weave between his. "I can do anything for a few hours."

He leaned closer. "I remember."

She gave him a side-eyed frown, but the menace wasn't there. Adrenaline raised her heart rate, the familiar drug coursing through her body. This was why she loved raids. The heady rush of superiority, of knowing she was in control and no one could stop her. After three years in a cage, she was free.

Kaleb's eyes gleamed with a devilish light. He winked at her.

Oh, yes, he felt it too. They had three hours to burn before they needed to break into the bowels of the station to destroy the primary power source for the nexus web. An Iloni couple strolled into sight and she snuggled a little closer to Kaleb, testing her acting skills to the limits. "Shall we go look around?" she asked in a syrupy sweet tone.

He grinned. "Dinner first, and then a leisurely stroll?"

"Are there any good restaurants here?"

"I know the perfect place."

The perfect place turned out to be Sensations, a restaurant on the lowest observatory level. They'd walked through station levels alive with music where Iloni frolicked without inhibition or clothes. But Sensations was virtually silent. Occasionally Lana caught the clink of fine crystal or the sound of footsteps, but otherwise the restaurant sat alone, cocooned in the sweeping vista of the stars.

A beautiful Iloni woman stood behind a podium near the entrance, while the rest of the dining area was swathed in gauzy veils, hiding the other diners from view. "Welcome to Sensations, where we feed your most sensual dreams. How many in your party?" She fluttered her lashes at Kaleb as she stepped out from behind the podium. In Lana's opinion, loose robes that looked like winding sheets shouldn't be allowed to be so sexy, but the woman's dress of ash-silver ribbons perfectly accented her hourglass body and wavy chocolate brown hair.

"Two," Kaleb said.

"Would you like any additions tonight?" The heated emotion in the woman's eyes said she was a breath away from stripping Kaleb down.

"No, thank you."

To Lana's surprise, the woman's smile widened. "Your room will be ready in a moment, sir." As she walked back to her podium Lana saw a thin strip of silver running up her forearm.

"Slave band," Kaleb whispered in her ear. "It's used on Iloni who have openly defied the Imperator or his rule." He lifted her hand to his lips. "It's in our future if we get caught."

A hot shiver of lust crawled up her arm as he kissed her hand. "That's the stick. What's my carrot?"

"Your own ship," Kaleb whispered.

A very good carrot. She almost asked if he came with the ship, but she killed that fantasy fast. They'd tried that once. This time she was sticking to her plan. She'd help Kaleb, get the crystals, and then get as far away from the rest of humanity as a good engine could take her.

"This way," the woman said. She led them through the flowing white silk veils to blue glass double doors that glowed like light under water. "Sir, your changing room is on the left. Sirra, your changing room is on the right. All of your clothing will be locked in the room during your dining experience."

"We're eating naked?" She shot Kaleb a look promising him a painful death.

"No, sirra, there are appropriate dining clothes in your changing room. Something more comfortable than the current fashion."

Lana nodded slowly. The red slash of the dress she was wearing certainly wasn't suitable for dining, but Kaleb's knowing grin made the whole thing suspect.

She stepped into the changing room and watched doubtfully as the door clicked behind her. The room was a muted gray with no obvious edges, no sound, and no smell. If nothing else, Prime had excellent air controls.

She stripped out of her dress and unfolded the pile of gauze, a little puff of pearlescent white that lay on the stone bench.

The cloth shimmered in the soft light like the nacre of an abalone shell, not truly gray or white, but catching all the colors of the rainbow while remaining true to none.

The pants were simple enough, loose and uncomplicated. After several tries she decided the top was meant to be a halter. It came with a thin matching sweater.

The outfit was comfortable, and about as sexy as the olive drab she'd worn shipside. At least that would get Kaleb to cool his engines. Checking to make sure her knife was well hidden in her boot heel, she left her own dress artfully rumpled on the bench, and stepped into the next room.

Kaleb was waiting for her in the egg-shaped room, seated on colorful cushions around a low black table. Cold air blew over her from an unseen vent.

Lana rubbed her covered arms. "If I'd known it was going to be this chilly, I would have brought my skirt in as a blanket."

"It'll get warmer," Kaleb said. "Sensations is all about contrast: hot and cold, smooth and rough. The meal is designed to appeal to each of your senses. It's supposed to be a very sensual experience."

She sank to her knees on the plush cushions across from him. "You've been here before?" Green-eyed jealousy roared like a rift dragon in the back of her mind. They'd been lovers, she reminded herself, not a bonded couple. They'd never talked of marriage or commitment. Less than a year together didn't make him hers.

"I've never been here," Kaleb said as the table made a soft whirring sound. "But I always wanted to come."

Two holes opened at the right side of the table and white mugs on saucers appeared. Steam rose from the cups with the scent of apple and cinnamon. Lana cupped her freezing hands around the welcome warmth.

Kaleb inhaled the steam before cautiously sipping the drink.

"Drugged?"

He shook his head. "Just hot. Sensations prides itself on not using any chemical supplements."

"Hmmm." She sipped the drink, crisp with the taste of apples, sultry cinnamon, and something sweet, maybe honey. The cider warmed her, pushing away the chill. For the first time all day, Lana smiled.

"Melithian cider." Kaleb lifted his glass again. "The apples grow only on a few peaks in the Melitine mountain range on Darrian 6, and the trees only bloom in frost. Blue blossoms over white snow, it's beautiful."

"You've seen it?"

"Only pictures." Kaleb shrugged, veering the conversation away from his past.

The table whirred again. This time a small red bowl appeared with a savory broth. Lana tasted her soup as silence stretched between them. History piled up in the wintry room with its blue-tinged walls. Everything she'd meant to say, everything they hadn't said, every dream of Kaleb dashing to her rescue.

She laughed humorlessly as she pushed the empty bowl away.

"What's so funny?"

"Those first few months as an Iloni prisoner, I kept waiting for you to rescue me. I imagined you running in with a raiding party to steal me away from there.

"The prison was pure hell. No light. No sound. Just endless darkness broken by irregular ration drops. After a few days you start hallucinating. I don't even know how long I was in there. It seemed like eternity, and then there was a bright light and someone talking at me. I barely understood it all, only that no one wanted to ransom me." Lana watched dispassionately as a plate of citrus-scented cookies appeared. "I blamed you. I wanted you to come and you didn't, so every day I cursed you. Because you weren't there." Tears threatened to roll down her cheeks, but she bit them back.

Kaleb reached across the table for her hand. "I thought you were dead. If I'd known, I would have come for you."

"I know. Geana showed me the recording of my funeral service while we were in transit. I think she was trying to apologize or something. She made me sit through all the footage of the bombings, the vid of my memorial. It was all a little… too much." She squeezed his hand once and dropped it. "I'm sorry I hated you all these years. I thought you'd abandoned me, that everyone had forgotten about me. The rest of the universe was spinning on happy and serene while I suffered. I never thought that maybe I was one of the lucky ones."

She turned away. The Iloni had tossed her in a lightless cell still wearing her ripped uniform. Bleeding, concussed, confused, they'd left her in a place where every sound echoed and there was no way to get warm. Sometimes, she'd thought she heard voices. After what seemed like years, the words turned to laughter. They were mocking her, and she'd heard Kaleb's mocking laughter with theirs.

The ordeal had become a blurry nightmare of shivering silence punctuated by the gnawing of her empty stomach. There was never enough food in prison. Apparently the Iloni saved all the excess for their own pleasures.

A vent blew warm air with a hint of wood smoke as the featureless floor turned into a wooden porch overlooking a vista of rolling hills and autumn forest. A single golden leaf fell beside her as tears welled in her eyes. She shook her head. It was over now. She was free. The Iloni weren't going to ruin any more of her life.

The main course was followed by a smaller course of shellfish and melted cheese with bread, and it seemed to Lana that as the meals got hotter, so did the room. It had been so cold when she'd entered, but now the steam from their dinner was turning the room into a sauna. She shucked her sweater, tossing it to the side, and Kaleb choked on something.

"Are you all right?" She glanced up from her plate, and froze. The humid air made his shirt stick to the sculpted muscles of his body. She took a deep breath, looking away as her imagination replayed the nights she'd spent worshipping his body, running her hands down his back as they made love.

Kaleb coughed again. She forced herself to look back. His eyes were riveted on her chest. She flushed with satisfaction and not a small amount of need. The past several weeks dancing around each other on the *Marsail* had only served to remind her of why she'd loved him in the first place.

She sighed, and he echoed it with one of his own. Undoubtedly he was remembering their time together, and what had ultimately driven them apart. Even if the Iloni hadn't captured her, their relationship was going to end. Kaleb had wanted to live dirtside; she'd wanted to be free to roam between the planets. The Apex War had forced him to live on a ship and her to go down into the gravity wells. In the end, the war was the only thing they had in common.

His gaze roamed over her body, lingering here and there, as his pupils widening with a hunger that food would never satisfy. "You're beautiful."

Her blood burned for his touch. For a moment, it was just the two of them in the universe. No expectations or responsibilities. No future or past. And she wanted him to touch her, to remind her how it felt to be truly alive. What it felt like to meld with another person until they were one.

A soft hum shook her out of her reverie. The cushions shuffled as the floor vibrated, and a small white tray appeared with six rows of small bowls, and two strips of black silk. "What is this?"

"Sight," Kaleb whispered in her ear, his hot breath tickling her neck. "Humans are visual creatures. We rely on what we see to influence our judgments. When we lose our vision, other senses are enhanced. We hear more, taste better, and our sense of touch is heightened." He brushed a kiss over the back of her neck. "You're supposed to blindfold your partner, and feed them. I'm told the element of surprise is very, very alluring."

She shivered in anticipation.

"Do you want to go first?"

She took a deep breath, feeling her nipples strain against the satiny fabric that clung to her body. "Yes."

For perhaps the second time in his life Kaleb wished he had some deity to curse. Lana sat in front of him—her body quivering, lips wet, and breasts highlighted by shimmering fabric that only accented her beautiful curves—and he was supposed to keep his pants on.

He finished tying the black blindfold around her eyes, fighting the urge to lean down and kiss her. She tilted her head back, a wanton invitation to taste her skin.

"What am I trying first?" Lana asked in a breathy whisper.

Kaleb shuddered with need. Stars above, he'd dreamt of that voice. In his dreams she'd found him in the darkness and made love to him. He leaned close, his lips almost caressing her ear. "It's a surprise."

Her lips curved in a tempting smile.

Patience. They had time. Maybe. If everything went right. He frowned down at the food and picked up one of the few he recognized: a luscious vanilla crème brûlée with a beautiful golden crust of caramelized sugar. Breaking the crust with a spoon, Kaleb scooped up a bite. "Open your mouth."

She giggled, and luscious pink lips parted.

Kaleb fed her the sweet custard. The lusty moan that escaped her lips fired his blood.

"Ooh. That's so good." She leaned forward. "More?"

He couldn't even find words. He fed her another bite. A smidgen of the crème brûlée remained on the corner of Lana's lip. Helpless to refuse, Kaleb leaned in and licked it away.

Lana's tongue darted out, brushing his lip.

The spoon dropped as he pulled Lana to him. He felt the heat of her palms as she grabbed his arm, then tangled her fingers in his hair. Their kiss turned desperate, as if a few moments could erase the years of pain and loss.

Kaleb fell backwards into the cushions. Lana followed, straddling him and brushing kisses down his neck. She pulled her blindfold off and grinned down at him. "I have a better idea for dessert."

"I love how you think." There was a small vibration by his knee, and Kaleb lifted his head in confusion. "What was that?"

Lana checked her ankle. "It's go time."

His head fell back into the soft pillows. They were the only thing soft at the moment. "Can we wait five more minutes?" He meant it as a joke, a way to get his mind back on the job, but blast the universe and his own inability to stop time. Once the Nova Crystals were in place, he was going to find an excuse to spend every minute with Lana.

"Five?" Lana said coolly. "What are you going to accomplish in five minutes?"

"I could maybe get your shirt off," he muttered as she stood up. The thin material of her outfit clung to her curves in the steamy room and he wanted to touch everything he saw. "Or my shirt off." Her eyes dropped to his chest and her tempting pink tongue darted out.

"You remember my weaknesses." She shook her head. "But we need to save the solar system, remember? This all runs on perfect timing. Let's just worry about surviving the next four hours, okay?"

The stealth suits Kaleb had smuggled in made it possible for them to slip out of Sensations without triggering any of the motion sensors, but did little to keep her warm in the narrow service passages meant for the slaves. Lana had to twist sideways to get past a row of pipes that protruded out into the passage. If Sensations had been the womb, the slave corridors were a crypt, cold and lifeless. Their footsteps echoed. If there was anyone in the halls, they were dead.

She turned to ask Kaleb where she should go, but the look of naked hunger on his face quelled her curiosity. They'd left dessert unfinished, much to her regret. A kiss was all it took to erase years of hate and fear. One perfect moment of happiness to treasure in the quiet years ahead.

"Next left," Kaleb said in a whisper that carried further than she wanted.

Lana wanted to look to Kaleb for reassurance, but she couldn't. Not now. Not knowing she had to give him up when they were done. If the buzzer on the clock hadn't gone off, there was no doubt in Lana's mind they would both be naked right now. A rush of heat and longing filled her, threatening her focus.

It had never been like this before. The raids they'd run together had been easy. They'd worked together, anticipating each other, moving in unison.

But they'd also been enjoying hot sex every moment they weren't fighting the Iloni.

Move on. When this is over he's going back to the Quintus fleet, and you're getting on a ship headed for the big black. Kiss him good-bye and let go.

"Quick, this is the hub we need." He dropped to one knee and pried up the deck plate. Twenty meters below, the primary energy source for the nexus web glittered like a diamond. They stared at it for a few silent heartbeats. "Are you sure about this? If there's an energy backlash—"

"I've done it before," Lana said. "Give me the toolkit. If you're worried about getting fried you can stay up top."

Kaleb held out the bag but he didn't let go.

"Give it to me. I know what I'm doing, Kaleb." She tugged at the tools. "We don't have time for this."

Dark eyes searched her face. "I love you, Lana. I don't want to lose you again."

She pulled the tools out of his hand. "Tell me that after we're past the rift." Lana dropped into the hole and shimmied down the ladder.

Blue light cast alien shadows along the mercurial wall around her. She could almost imagine voices—whispers of the dead.

Nexus webs were strange things, nets of energy beams that defied every law of physics as she understood it, but they worked because of the energy source. A primary source on one end—always blue—and the secondary source on the far end glowing orange.

In between the two batteries, a rainbow of light created an unbreakable cage. The Nova Crystals hung in that cage, all their life-giving energy trapped in an unimaginably long necklace of light.

With a final eight foot drop, Lana landed on the narrow platform beside the energy source.

"Trouble?" Kaleb's voice echoed from above.

"Not yet." She took a deep breath.

Either she was missing something, or the Iloni were truly as arrogant as the outworlders always said. She couldn't see any security locks. No palm reader, not even a number pad beside the locks.

"Lana?"

"Where's the security?"

"On the door." The exasperation in his voice was clear.

Lana looked behind the power source at the catwalk that stretched across the chamber to a door. "But there's a ladder by the door. It isn't secure."

"This ladder is for the slaves, who have implants to prevent them from doing what we're doing. On the other side of that door is a ceremonial room with very live guards who will kill us very dead if they see us. Do you want me to open the door for you?" Kaleb asked.

She shook her head no.

"Thought not. Let's just get this done. Geana's team will be moving the ship in three minutes, if they aren't dead."

A shiver of terror ran up her spine. For a moment, she was alone again, trapped in the vast blackness of space with no back up and no hope. The panic swelled, threatening to drown her.

Kaleb dropped down beside her.

She shook the panic attack away. "You're supposed to be standing guard."

"I am."

Lana rolled her eyes. "If someone comes down that hall I'd like to know about it before they lock us in and vent the oxygen."

"We'll hear anyone coming long before they get close. You could hear a flea breathe the way those tunnels echo."

"I'll take your word for it. The rift is blissfully parasite free. Except for the Iloni." She pulled the cover off the power box and eyed the thick wires. "A T-64, you think? Let's try that." Digging through the bag of adaptors for every occasion—including a hideously outdated M-mod which must have been thrown in out of desperation—she found the adaptor. A folded piece of paper clung to a sticky edge.

"Um…" Kaleb bent to retrieve the paper.

Lana snatched it away and unfolded it with a snap of her wrist. Delicate calligraphy curled across the page forming elegant "wherefores" and "by thy leaves" that ended with Kaleb's assumed name and signature next to her name and a blank. "You brought the fake marriage certificate but didn't have me sign it?"

"I was going to ask—"

"Never mind." She crumpled the paper and stuffed it in her pocket. "We'll talk about it later. Honestly, you used to be better with planning details." She took out the energy reader and carefully connected it to the white wire. "Stand back. If I start screaming, don't do what I did." A flick of her thumb, and the power reader showed two charges, one for the power leech and one for the primary energy source. Shipboard, power surges were life-threatening. Lightning between the clouds of the rift was common enough, and one hit could leave a ship tumbling blind through the asteroid belt that divided the inner and outer worlds.

She plugged the leech into the reader and turned the control on. Green lights danced across the screen. "Primary energy source at ninety-seven percent. Ninety-four. Ninety."

"Too fast," Kaleb said. "You'll set off an alarm if you aren't careful."

"Eighty-four." She turned the leech down. "Eighty-three. Time?"

"Ninety seconds until Geana is scheduled to break from the dock."

"I wish we knew if the secondary source was leeched already. Seventy-eight."

Kaleb moved closer, the heat of his body warming her. "We'll know as soon as all hell breaks loose. If there aren't sirens going off within the next five minutes, something's wrong."

"Did we make a fall back plan? Seventy-five."

She felt his hand on the small of her back as he tried to peek over her shoulder at the read out. "Shoot everyone?"

"Why do your back-up plans always involve killing everyone?"

"It's effective?"

"Fifty-nine. Forty. Thirty. Ten percent drain, it's switching to the back-up and recharging." She turned the leech off. "If the secondary source is at forty, we have seven minutes before the nexus web collapses and the Nova Crystals plummet to the planet's surface."

"And six minutes to get to the shuttle pads. Up the ladder."

Lana rolled the tools up and climbed back to the slave passages as the blue light below her began to fade. "I really hope Geana picked up that shuttle in time. I am going to hate myself if those crystals smash somewhere other than the outer planets."

"But think of all the fun the Iloni would have trying to live on a terraforming planet! I bet they'd make new Nova Crystals."

"Bet you they wouldn't since the likelihood of surviving that kind of terraforming is…yeah, I don't think you can. We may have just killed everyone."

"Geana's a pirate. You can trust a pirate. Two rights, and the third left. Run." Every stray sound echoed, including Kaleb's harsh curse as they heard boot steps behind them. "Keep going."

"Whatever happens," Kaleb whispered. "Don't stop. Whatever happens to me, get out."

Boot steps clattered up behind them. "Stop! This is a privileged area. Identify yourselves."

Kaleb halted, pushing Lana behind him as he turned.

The guard stopped a few feet away. He was dressed in utilitarian gray worker's clothes. Iloni, like everyone else on Prime, but with something familiar about him. *I know him from somewhere.*

"Hello, Adrian."

Lana nearly tripped over her feet. "Adrian?" she asked in a whisper. "You know someone here?"

The man scowled and raised a gun. "Kaleb. I didn't realize you were back in the Imperator's good graces."

Kaleb caught her hand and squeezed it once. "His whims and favors change with the wind, Adrian. Everyone knows that."

"You know the Imperator?" Lana muttered in his ear.

"I met him once," Kaleb admitted, just as quietly. Louder he said, "I didn't think I'd get a chance to see you this visit."

"Did you come to kill me? That was the Imperator's requirement if you wanted to remain on Darrian 6, wasn't it?" Adrian asked.

Kaleb shrugged.

Adrian turned his gun on Lana. "Who is she?"

"Lana, my love, meet Adrian. Adrian, say hello to Lana si Vera."

The muscle under Adrian's eye twitched. Lana shrunk behind Kaleb's shoulder. "You are far too calm, Kaleb. We need to run from the guy with the gun. And then you're going to explain all of this. In detail."

Kaleb squeezed her hand. "He won't shoot his brother."

"You have a brother?" Lana asked. "An Iloni brother?"

"It's not that surprising," Kaleb said. "I am Iloni, after all."

Adrian growled. "Did you come here to finish it? A trip to Prime with your wife as a reward for killing me? Is that all it took to bribe you?" He eyed Lana. "Which family is she from anyway?"

Kaleb gripped her hand tighter.

"I'm from the rift," Lana said.

Adrian's eyebrows went up. "That's what rift rats look like? I expected something shriveled and pale, like a dead albino rat."

Alarms screamed. The lights dimmed to a cold white as the station tried to repower the dead energy source for the nexus web.

Lana tugged on Kaleb's arm. "We need to go."

"Adrian, come with us." Kaleb held out his hand. "Come with me."

"To where?" Adrian looked between them in confusion. "What is going on, little brother?"

"We're rebuilding the outworlds."

"Impossible."

"Not once we take the Nova Crystals." Kaleb nodded at the gun. "Are you going to shoot us, or come with us?"

Adrian shifted, and a long silver bar on his forearm caught the light. "No matter my choice, I am the Imperator's. I can't leave my assigned area without dying." Silence stretched between them as the alarms gargled to a halt. "Go. Go!" Adrian waved at them. "The shuttle in dock 3C is our long range scout, take her."

Without warning Kaleb stepped forward and hugged his brother. "I'll come back for you. I'll find a way!" He took Lana's hand again. "Our ship's waiting."

Lana watched a tendril of rift smoke as it curled past the window of the shuttle. Her head hurt. Sixteen hours of piloting the shuttle and running interference for Geana's ship while Kaleb manned the guns had left her desperate for sleep. "Rift cleared," she announced over the comms. "We're as safe as we're going to get."

On the radar she could see the line of outworlds ships arranged to defend the *Marsail* and the Nova Crystals against the Iloni pursuit. The first Apex War had left few long range vessels on either side, but even one Iloni long range cruiser on this side of the rift was one too many. "Fifteen? So few? And what's that, the *Apollo*? She's not a war cruiser!" The outworlders had brought a hospital ship to their defense. Its only option for battle was to ram the enemy vessel, but she knew they would. To protect the Nova Crystals, they would do anything.

She heard Kaleb coming into the cockpit behind her.

"So, you're pure blood Iloni?" she asked nonchalantly. She sent a burst message, announcing their arrival to the waiting ships.

He sat down in the co-pilot's seat. "Does it matter?"

She wasn't sure. "Who else knows?"

"No one," he said. "At first no one cared. I was someone with military experience and I was on their side. And then there never seemed to be the right moment to tell anyone."

"Before we met your brother would have been a good time," she said.

"I didn't think we'd run into him." Kaleb winced. "I'd meant to explain it to you eventually. I was going to tell you, I just didn't know how." He fell silent, watching her.

Lana set the shuttle on auto-pilot. "We should reach Quintus territory in three days. If the third team did their job, our pick up will be waiting." She stood, stretching, and avoiding Kaleb's eyes. "I'm going to sleep."

"Do you hate me?"

She rounded on him. "You lied to me. You lied to everyone. You're not an outworlder at all. You aren't one of us." Tears welled in her eyes. "Was anything you ever said true?"

"I was born the second son of the di Vera family. Adrian went to the military academy. There were riots, and he refused to fire at a pregnant woman. The Imperator called him in front of the entire court and dragged the woman in as well. Adrian had to choose between killing her or forfeiting his life. He wouldn't shoot her."

Lana crossed her arms. "That's Adrian. What did *you* do?"

"The Imperator called on my family to redeem our name. I was the heir. In front of the court I was told to murder my brother or be erased from the Iloni records of life. I walked out. I took the first shuttle I could find to the rift and worked my way as a ship hand until I arrived on Quintus. I had military experience and information about Iloni troops. No one asked how."

"Why didn't you tell me? Everyone else, I can understand. But I thought we had something more. In all that time together, every time I asked about your past, why didn't you say something?"

He shook his head. "I was scared that you'd leave me."

"You were right. I *am* leaving you. We want different things. We come from different worlds. All I've ever wanted was to have someone who was always going to be there for me. I want a ship, a crew I can trust, and someone to come with me. You… I don't even know what you want. I thought I knew you, and now you're making me question everything." She glared at him.

Kaleb shrunk in on himself, crossed arms becoming a protective huddle. "I didn't lie to you. I just left a few things out of the conversation."

Lana pointed an accusing finger at him. "When you arrived at Prime, you used your real name. Not Kaleb Hath, but an Iloni name. That's still you. And you never told me." She shook her head. "You're great in bed, Kaleb. I missed that. If we'd had more time at Prime I would have enjoyed having you again. But let's be honest, what we had was a lie. And now it's over."

He looked away. "This isn't what I wanted our reunion to be."

"Then maybe you should have told me the truth." She walked away. The door to her berth didn't slam when she shut it, but once inside she hit her hand against the unforgiving metal. "Damn you, Kaleb. Why do you do this to me?" Why did he have to be Iloni, the bastard. And why did it hurt so much to walk away?

Three awkward days of avoided conversation and eight weeks of Quintus hospitality had worn Lana's patience to the bone.

Quintus, the fifth planet from the sun and the closet to the rift, was nothing like she remembered. The great clouds that had held the flying cities aloft had been blown away by Iloni warships in the last months of the war. There was little more than a heavy core of molten metal at the bottom of a crushing gravity well, and a decimated fleet orbiting the wreckage.

Every ship she'd been on was packed with refugees. They lined the halls, slept in the galleys, crowded the cargo bays. She'd wondered how Kaleb was going to make good on his promise to give her a ship, or if he'd even try. But he'd left a message for her the night before. Nothing elaborate, just the docking bay number of the giant *Titan*-class vessel *Solace*.

Lana shoved her stealth suit into the duffel with more force than necessary. Damn thing wouldn't fit.

It wasn't like she'd expected Kaleb to beg her forgiveness; she'd made it clear he wouldn't get it. But that was Kaleb's MO, always coming back, forever at the back of her mind, even on the days she hated him.

She pulled the suit back out and smoothed it flat. Her fingers ran over a bump, and she pulled a crumpled document out of the pocket. The marriage certificate. She snorted. Now, there was an idea. She could sign it and make it legally binding. Wouldn't Kaleb just die? The idiot hadn't even managed to write the correct date on it.

Of course, he'd have to leave Quintus, and even before her capture that had been a sticking point. *He* wanted to stay and the thought of tying herself to a gravity well had made *her* ill. Bad idea. She folded the document and tucked it in her pocket.

With a sigh, she trudged down the hall to docking bay four, a monstrous hangar large enough to house a small armada, and with room enough to swallow the mining station she'd been born on.

Lana wound through the maze of mismatched shuttles and merchant vessels until she saw Kaleb standing by a deep space scout.

"Lana." He held out a sheaf of papers and unlocked the ramp so it slowly extended. "*Spiral*-class vessel 11-A12. She needs a name, but she's yours."

She followed him up into the ship. Dust swirled around their feet as they walked through the stale air. "Does the environmental system work?"

"It does, I checked it this morning. The previous captain docked her here prior to running a raid with the Quintus military before the end of the war. He didn't make it back, and until now no one had an interest in taking this vessel out." He pointed down the corridor to a red door. "The secondary cargo bay is equipped for mine hauling in the rifts, and the guns are over-sized Taxons. If you can't outrun it, you can out shoot anything short of an Iloni warship. She's registered out of Quintus, but flagged for welcome anywhere on the Outer Planets. I added Iloni registration as well; Darrian 3. I hope you'll never need it, but if you decide to run raids the patrols shouldn't give you any trouble."

She stepped onto the small bridge, checked the control boards, then turned her attention to the papers Kaleb had handed her. "There's an order in for new computers? Why?"

"The ship used to have a full crew. Max capacity is eight, unless you double bunk, but she needs a minimum of two to run right now. The *Solace* isn't exactly overflowing with supplies, so I put in the work order. As soon as one of the raids nets the components you need, you'll be supplied with the upgrade to turn her into a one-man ship."

Lana frowned, but nodded. The Quintians were giving her more than she felt comfortable asking for already. "Right."

"Everyone in the outworlds is very grateful for what you did. The first Nova Crystals have dropped, and we're seeing the first signs of organic growth on Quintus and Triell. You'll be a hero everywhere you go."

Lana ignored the second-hand praise. "Am I stuck here until the computer parts come in?" Everything else appeared to be up to spec; better than she'd hoped for really. With a ship like this she could do anything. Her heart raced with fear. That's what she'd wanted, right? She'd planned on building a ship in the waste hauler, and now Kaleb was just handing her one, and that was good… Very good, she told herself as she locked her fears away. There was nothing wrong with being alone.

"No, you won't be stuck here. We've arranged a copilot for you."

"A co-pilot?" Her heart skipped a beat.

"Someone who won't be missed if you decide to space him." Kaleb's serious tone made her look up.

She raised an eyebrow. "That's not a funny joke."

"It's not a joke at all." His expression dared her to doubt him.

A co-pilot would expand her options. With a ship, she could open some new trade routes or run some raids. The possibilities unfolded in her mind until she quashed it with a heavy dose of reality. Kaleb wasn't giving her a crew; he was giving her someone the rest of the station hoped would die in vacuum. Hard reality killed her daydreams. "How bad *is* this guy?"

Kaleb shrugged, and looked at the floor.

She growled at his reticence, and flipped through the rest of the paperwork. "It looks good. She's fueled up?"

"Yes."

One word answers now? Lana scanned another page, pursing her lips as she wrangled in her temper. "My gear's loaded?"

"Yes, it's in the captain's berth, waiting for you."

Suspicion bit her, hard. Kaleb wasn't stupid enough to let a stranger wander the ship to load gear. "Who is this co-pilot?"

"No one important," Kaleb said, in a perfectly bland voice. She knew that one. That was Kaleb trying to play innocent.

She narrowed her eyes. "*You're* my co-pilot?"

Kaleb shrugged.

"Stars above." Lana rubbed her eyes. "Are you out of your ever-lovin' mind?"

"My name is Kaleb Hatheron di Vera, second born and heir to the di Vera family of Darrian 6. Twenty-sixth in line for the throne of the Imperator from my mother's side. I'm a qualified deep space pilot, engineer, and gunner. I have a decade of military experience, and six months of mining experience."

"Mining?" Lana asked in disbelief. "What were you doing mining? You could have got yourself killed!"

Another shrug. "Mining the rift was the only way to bring in enough water for the refugees."

She couldn't stop her eyes from rolling. "Kaleb, you're not a co-pilot, you're a hero missing his quest! Go find your beautiful damsel in distress and your happily ever after already." She slammed the papers down on the command consul.

"I did. I found you. I lost you. And I won't lose you again, not without a fight, not without you telling me that I'm not who you want."

Lana shot him a look, but the glare that had once made soldiers quiver in terror bounced right off Kaleb.

"Give me three months."

"And then?" She raised an eyebrow.

"If you want, you can shove me out the airlock."

"Fine. But I will shove you out the airlock if you annoy me. This is my ship now." She glared at him a moment longer.

"Any time, Captain."

She pulled the marriage certificate out of her pocket. "Do you remember this?"

Kaleb eyed it with suspicion. "I do."

"You got the date wrong, you know."

"No. I didn't. It was the date I had it written."

Lana held the paper at arm's length. "You had this written up before I was captured?"

"Before the Battle of Prenta. I had it all planned out, an elaborate meal, I think I had a speech worked out. There might have been poetry. And then the alarms went off, we were caught in an ambush, and I barely saw you between that and… and when I lost you."

Lana hesitated. She wasn't sure she would have agreed to marriage three years ago, back when staying with him would have seemed like the perfect path to a broken heart. Having lived without Kaleb once, though, she knew what to do: she signed the paper. "There now. All official. If I throw you out the airlock I also get your death gratuity from the Quintian military."

"Whatever you say, Captain."

Her lips softened into a smile. "We'll see if you're still saying that after you've spent a week with me in command."

Kaleb's hand slipped around her waist. "Have I ever told you how sexy you look when you're giving me orders, Captain?"

She snuggled closer. "So, if I ordered you to the captain's cabin and told you to strip, would that work for you?"

"I could make it work for both of us." Kaleb brushed his lips against her forehead.

"Oh?" Her question turned into a mewl of half-hearted protest as Kaleb continued his exploration down the side of her neck.

"Does my captain still…"

She gasped with pleasure as he nuzzled the sensitive skin of her shoulder.

Kaleb chuckled. "You *do* still like that." He scooped her up and carried her down the hall to the captain's cabin. "Permission to strip the captain, Captain?"

"Permission granted."

ABOUT THE AUTHOR

Liana Brooks is probably human. At least, she claims to be human. There's a rumor going around that she's part shark, and she has an uncanny understanding of spaceship engines. Still, we'll allow that she's probably human, and the tracking device we attached indicates she's still in North America. For now. She has a tendency to wander, the poor dear.

STORY INSPIRATION

Where do story ideas come from anyway? I think they're made of starlight and moonbeams. You walk out on the front porch on a crisp autumn night and see the Milky Way shimmering in the heavens full of promise… and the next thing you know there's a story rambling through your head. Lana was born on such a night, when shooting stars lit up bright red autumn leaves. Kaleb followed, as he always does, because where would the prince be without his rift rat?

FREE EBOOK

Thank you for buying this book!

When you buy an Inkprint Press book in print, we like to thank you by offering you the ebook for free. Please head to:

http://www.inkprintpress.com/liana-brooks/prime-sensations/

And use the coupon PRIMEPRINT to download your free copy in both .mobi and .epub formats. (The coupon will only work once.)

BODIES IN MODTION

Newton's Laws Book #1

A civil war tore them apart. Can a cold war bring them back together?

Available from all major retailers.

BODIES IN MOTION
Newton's Laws #1

CHAPTER 1

THE PROBLEM WITH VACATIONS, Selena reflected as she adjusted her sweater outside Cargo Blue, was that reality was always waiting at the end.

A quick search of the local security cameras found one that showed the peeling sunburn on her right shoulder blade. Such was the curse of pale-skinned, ship-born Fleet personnel. Anytime she left the foggy belts covering the city of Tarrin, she barbecued like a shrimp, no matter how much sunscreen she applied. Otherwise, she'd flee even further from the Fleet Enclave and make her home on the equatorial beaches of the planet they were trapped on.

She panned the camera and checked her left shoulder. Black ink made a starscape that disguised three silver scars as shooting stars. The painting covered her shoulder blade and part of her upper arm. As the artist had promised, the skin-paint had kept her from burning as much, though it still had the over-stretched feel of a burn. With a few adjustments, her uniform covered most of the temporary art; it would keep her from having to explain to her colleagues.

Her forearm warmed, a warning that someone was about to contact her through the tech implant tucked between her radius and ulna.

She hesitated too long and the call came through, a persistent ping against her skull as the phantom image of her best friend floated on the edge of her vision.

Selena turned off the visual receiver and answered. "Genevieve," she said with a smile as the image of her vivacious, red-headed friend appeared floating against the backdrop of landing gear that supported the grounded fleet.
A grounder would have thought she was talking to herself, but grounders wouldn't set foot near the neo-city-state of Enclave. The rocky beach served as a city and tomb for the survivors of the last war.

"Selena!" Gen gushed. "Starcom to Selena. Where are you? I'm covering for now."

"Delayed, but almost there." Selena hoped Gen wouldn't hear the lie. She'd been standing in the shadows of the Enclave pub for nearly a quarter of an hour.

"The *Lorenza* could get here faster," Gen said, referencing a long-dead ship whose crew were found skeletonized at their stations. Gen blew hair off her face. "Stars above, you're an hour late. The whole fleet is flying faster than you."

Selena turned on her visual long enough to roll her eyes at her friend. "Ha, ha, funny. That joke needs to be forcibly retired." Sooner rather than later. The fleet couldn't fly without fuel, and the Malik system they were stranded in held precious few deposits of the orun crystals needed to power the ships.

"If you don't come," Gen said threateningly, "I will teleport to your apartment and drag you out in your pajamas."

"I'm not at home," Selena admitted. And she wouldn't have let her best friend come to her new house if she was.

Gen was smart enough to realize that the small palace Selena had bought in downtown Tarrin wasn't paid for by her official OIA salary. The paygrades for the Office of Imperial Affairs had last been updated when the Malik system was still in contact with the empire, making them 900 years out of date.

Technically, taking a second job wasn't treason, but there were enough people in the fleet who'd see it as a betrayal that keeping it secret felt right. Especially since Gen's captain would scream the loudest.

Gen clapped. "Selena! Stop stalling yer engines and get in here. This isn't some Fleet Tribunal, just our friends. You, me, Carver. I left a message for Marshall. You know. People we like."

The light of understanding dawned. "Carver? This is so you can snuggle up to Perrin Carver without your parents watching?"

"Yes," Gen admitted, not looking the least bit contrite.

"You're only dragging me along so I can cover for you while you make out in a corner, aren't you?" She masked the relief with mock anger. At least Gen wasn't trying to set Selena up with one of her cousins. Or, ancestors forbid, Gen's handsy older brother.

Again.

Gen opened her eyes wide with an innocent smile. "Maybe."

"Gen!" Selena rolled her eyes. "Doesn't he have his own place?"

"Just the bachelor's dorm. The Carvers didn't have any ships except the shuttle his parents crashed in. Making out next door to Mom and Dad? No. And the BOQ? It's so tacky. You can hear everything through those walls."

Selena hid a smile. "I'll be there soon enough."

If Gen ever caught wind of how panicky the thought of a relationship made her, Gen would make it her life's goal to see Selena paired off. And there wasn't a man alive who she could imagine getting close to now.

Her implant pulled up an image of a tall, broad-shouldered, lean-muscled fighter with skin black as the night between stars and emerald-green eyes.

She pushed the memory away.

Lieutenant Commander Titan Sciarra was striking, intelligent, and had a body she'd cross battle lines for, but he was also out of reach. There was no point in chasing a man who wouldn't give her the time of day.

Another crew shuffled past her into the bar, black patches with silver fists on their shoulders.

It was getting harder to pretend she belonged in Enclave, with the fleet. Once upon a time, she'd known every crew's patch without thinking. She could name captains, their ships and their seconds by rote. Now she'd need to tap into the fleet's information nexus if she wanted to know who they were.

She stopped at the edge of the door to tug her lightest shields into place. A few minor adjustments would keep bugs away, keep beer off her clothes, and prevent anyone from hacking into her implant. They could still send messages, because disallowing that would have raised eyebrows.

And they could still hit her. But she could always hit back.

Selena rolled her shoulders and strutted into Cargo Blue. It was a battlefield, but she was the last captain of the Caryll family, and she wasn't going down without a fight.

Whatever crew owned Cargo Blue probably hadn't had much of a decorating budget, but at least they'd stuck with a theme: oversized cargo boxes were piled up to make walls, seating, and tables.

Olive-green safety webbing draped from the ceiling between blue lights. Fog used for fire drills on the ships pumped across the floor to hide the concrete beneath.

There was no bouncer at the door, but people were still hanging around the entrance.

As a rule, the fleet was cautious, and the young faces she saw belonged to fleet members who had never ventured outside their own crew more than a few times, even though the fleet had been grounded for nearly three years.

Tables to the left, bar ahead, dance floor to the right... and that meant the back half of the cargo hanger had been partitioned and karaoke would be in the back right corner. After a few minutes of weaving through the human crush, she found Gen, already sitting in Perrin Carver's lap and giggling.

"Selena!" Gen jumped up and hugged her. "I was beginning to worry!"

"How many people are in here?" Selena shouted over the music.

"Everyone under forty?" Gen laughed. With a small hand wave Gen put up a minor sound shield, muting the music. "People are going to stir crazy. Combine that with the anniversary—"

The anniversary.

Today.

The day the war had begun, the day the united fleet had died.

They'd been dying for four hundred years, well aware that the reserve of orun crystals was depleted and there was no way to move forward with the ships they had.

Old Captain Baular had seen the deposit of orun on the fifth planet as their saving grace. He'd get it even if it meant killing the grounders. And, coward that he was, he'd ordered his grandson to lead the first attack instead of leading it himself.

That opening skirmish began and ended in the dark, with Titan Sciarra in the infirmary, and five Aca-demy fighters missing or damaged. But by lunch of the next day, every officer belonging to crews allied with the Baulars withdrew.

Seven months later, heated words turned to live rounds.

"Selena?" Gen asked quietly, placing a hand on her arm. "You didn't know the date, did you?"

"I was trying not to think about." If she had, she'd have cut her vacation to the islands early.

Maybe even made her pilgrimage to the small cay where she'd ditched her stolen fighter after driving off the attack.

She rolled her shoulder, stretching the deep scars. "It snuck up on me."

"First round, we drink to the Lost Fleet, and all who've gone on to crew it. I'm buying," Gen said with a touch of forced joviality. "Carver's been making friends. Tell her, babe." She pushed Carver's shoulder.

Perrin Carver was tall, broad-shouldered man with shy, hazel eyes that hid a wicked sense of humor.

Selena's heart fluttered just a little at the memory of a time when she'd fancied herself in love with him. He'd been the ideal starsider: intelligent, good-looking, and charismatic. They'd been friends of a sort, but even that relationship had soured when she'd realized he'd been getting close to her so he could learn more about Genevieve Silar.

Carver nodded and held out his hand. "Hi, Selena. How are you?"

She tapped the back of his hand with hers, letting him test her shields. "Good. How's the Starguard?"

"Booming." The commander of the Starguard smiled, white teeth flashing, but there was a tightness around his eyes. "Everyone hears about guardians being allowed outside the Enclave, or working with the Jhandarmi, and I'm drowning in recruiting requests. Captains of larger crews invite me to Captain's Mess so they can introduce me to their best and brightest. Half the time I can't tell if they want me to marry into the crew or take the fleetlings into the guard." His shield was still attached to hers, scanning her as he talked.

All he would get from her was polite interest. Her heartrate didn't spike or dip at the mention of the Jhandarmi. Her smile never flickered.

"Maybe you should lock down Gen," Selena said. "If you had a spouse, no one would try to get you to marry into the crew."

Carver and Gen shared a look, and Gen sent a ping of information that Selena's implant translated as an ongoing debate over crew name and a place to live.

Carver sent something similar; a picture of his bachelor's quarters and his one ship. There was no room for them to marry and have a family.

"Enclave is a temporary solution," Selena said out loud. She'd lost the taste for communicating by implant years ago. "If we—"

A heavy hand wrapped around her waist as someone wearing too much cologne stepped far too close to her. "Hello, Selena."

Hollis Silar, one of Gen's many siblings, kissed her temple.

Selena sighed, sending a shock through her shield to Hollis's hand and elbowing him in the gut at the same time. "Hi, Hollis. I see you're still bathing in cologne rather than water."

He stepped away from her, an easy smile still in place.

It wasn't that Hollis was bad looking; plenty of women found him handsome. It was that he was equally affectionate with every woman he saw and he couldn't keep a secret to save his life. Or anyone else's. He'd chase anyone with a pretty smile and fell in and out of love a couple of times a day.

"Nice to see you too, Selena. Now, everyone, you're all going to look at me, smile, and laugh like I'm my normal, dashing self," he said, his smile never changing. "You haven't been paying attention, but I'm not a member of the Starguard for nothing. We're being watched. Now take your nice drinks from the waitress and keep your eyes on me."

Hollis nodded to the waitress and handed out four cups with bright purple liquid. "Bruised Stars all around. Guaranteed to make you giggle, or so the guy at the bar told me. Although he's a Seutaai, so take it with a shield in place." He handed Selena her drink with a smile, but turned immediately to glance over his shoulder.

"Big brother, who are we looking for?" Gen asked with a slow drawl. "Is it a friend who you might have forgotten to call back after a night out?"

Hollis shook his head. "No, I thought I saw some of the Lee crew. Make that, I'm certain of it."

Selena grimaced. "As long as Rowena isn't here."

"Did you call me?"

Startled, Selena looked up to the face of her least favorite woman: Rowena Lee. "Hello," Selena said politely. "I see you're still alive. That's…" *Unfortunate.* She nodded and took a slug of her Bruised Star.

Rowena held up a tray of electric blue shots. "My crew thinks I can't out-drink anyone in this bar. I probably can't go toe-to-toe with alcoholics like the Silars here. But No-Shot Selena?" Rowena set the drinks on the table. "I can out-shoot you in the stars or on the ground."

Gen sucked in air between her teeth and sent Selena several urgent pings telling her to ignore the Lees.

Selena muted Gen. "I took plenty of shots in the war. As I recall, I disabled three of your big birds. *Bassi, Aryton, Theoano…* Bang, bang, bang." Selena mimed firing with her finger. "Three shots. Three silent ships."

"Not kills," Rowena said. "A whole war and you never blooded yourself."

That was it, the memory she didn't want to face; the time she'd almost taken Death's claim and risked killing someone outside of war.

"That's uncalled for," Hollis said, trying to step between them. "Selena, why don't we—"

Selena pushed Hollis aside and grabbed the first shot. She tossed back the potent drink and shattered the glass on the table. "Go suck vacuum, Rowena. You're a pissant yeoman with no hope of command."

"I went to the Academy, same as you, Selena. I fought for the fleet." Rowena slammed a shot back.

"You fought for the mud-lickers."

Selena took another shot as the first started to fuzz her judgement. "I prevented the Baulars from committing mass genocide and destroying the civilians along with the fleet."

Rowena took her second shot. A crowd was gathering and that seemed to feed her cruelty. "The Lees survived the war. We're still here. How many Caryll captains are there? Oh, right, one. Can you count that high, No-Shot? You have any idea how easy it would be for me to end you right now?"

Selena took the last two glasses and slammed them both back.

Gen pinged her, giving locations, counts, and identities of the Lee allies in the crowd.

Hollis stepped to her flank, ready to defend her. She stood, anger burning through her veins. "Sure, your crew outnumbers mine. I guess on paper, it's not really a fair fight, is it, Rowena? But you were trained as a flight leader, and what do Carylls do? Hand-to-hand combat. Maybe I should thin your ranks, starting with one mouthy yeoman."

Keep reading! Buy now from your favorite retailer at: http://www.lianabrooks.com/bodies-in-motion/

THE DAY BEFORE
Time & Shadows Book #1

A dead body is found in the Alabama wilderness. Is it a human corpse… or just a piece of discarded property?

Available from all major retailers.
http://www.lianabrooks.com/books/time-shadows/

EVEN VILLAINS FALL IN LOVE
Heroes & Villains Book #1

Can a super villain at the top of his game drop everything to save the woman he loves?

Available from all major retailers.
http://www.lianabrooks.com/books/heroesand
villains/